THE NIGHTINGALE

Hans Christian Andersen's

THE
NIGHTINGALE

TRANSLATED BY

Eva Le Gallienne

DESIGNED AND ILLUSTRATED BY NANCY EKHOLM BURKERT

✶✶ HARPER & ROW, PUBLISHERS ✶ NEW YORK ✶ EVANSTON ✶ LONDON ✶✶

THE NIGHTINGALE

IN CHINA,

you know, the Emperor is Chinese, and all his subjects are Chinese too. This all happened many years ago, but for that very reason the story should be told. It would be a pity if it were forgotten.

THE EMPEROR had the most beautiful palace in all the world. It was built of the finest porcelain and had cost a fortune, but it was so delicate and fragile you had to be very careful how you moved about in it.

The garden was full of exquisite flowers; on the rarest and most beautiful, tiny silver bells were hung, so that people passing by would be sure to notice them. Indeed, everything in the Emperor's garden had been most ingeniously planned,

1

and it was so large that the gardener himself didn't know the full extent of it. If you kept on walking long enough, you came to a wonderful forest with great trees and fathomless lakes. The forest grew all the way down to the deep blue sea; the trees stretched their branches over the water, and large ships could sail right under them. Here lived a nightingale who sang so sweetly that even the poor fisherman—who had so much else to attend to—would stop and listen to her as he drew in his nets at night. "How beautiful that is!" he would say; then he had to get back to his work and forget about the bird. But the next night when he came to tend his nets and heard her singing, he would say again, "How beautiful that is!"

Travelers from all over the world came to the Emperor's city. They were filled with admiration for it, and for the palace and the garden. But when they heard the Nightingale, they all exclaimed, "That's the loveliest thing of all!"

When they returned home the travelers told all about their visits, and the scholars wrote many books describing the city, the palace, and the garden—but not one of them forgot the Nightingale; they kept their highest praise for her. And those who could write poetry wrote exquisite poems about the Nightingale who lived in the forest by the deep blue sea.

These books went all over the world, and at last some of them reached the Emperor. He sat in his gold chair reading and reading, every now and then nodding his head with pleasure when he came to an especially magnificent description of his city, his palace, and his garden. "But the Nightingale is the loveliest thing of all!" the books said.

"What's this?" cried the Emperor. "The Nightingale? I've never heard of her! To think that there is such a bird in my Empire—in my very own garden—and no one has told me about her! I have to read about her in a book! It's positively disgraceful!"

So he sent for his Chamberlain, who was so very haughty that if anyone of inferior rank dared to address him or ask him a question, he only deigned to answer, "Peh!"—which of course means nothing at all!

"I understand there is a highly remarkable bird here called the Nightingale," said the Emperor. "They say she is the loveliest thing in my whole Empire! Why has no one told me about her?"

"I've never heard that name before," answered the Chamberlain. "She's not been presented at Court, I'm sure of that."

"I want her to come here this very evening and sing for me!" said the Emperor. "It seems the whole world knows that I possess this marvel, yet I myself know nothing about her!"

"No! I have never heard that name!" the Chamberlain repeated. "But I shall look for her, and most certainly shall find her!"

But where was he to look?

He ran up and down all the staircases, through all the halls and corridors, asking everyone he met about the Nightingale—but no one knew anything about her. At last he ran back to the Emperor and told him it must be some fantastic story invented by the people who write books. "Your Imperial Majesty shouldn't pay attention to everything that's written down. It's mostly pure imagination—what we call black magic!"

"But I read this in a book sent me by the High and Mighty Emperor of Japan—therefore it must be true! I insist on hearing the Nightingale. She must be here this very evening! I am graciously inclined toward her—and if you fail to produce her you'll all get your stomachs punched immediately after supper!"

"Tsing-peh!" cried the Chamberlain, and he started running again, up and down the staircases, through all the halls and corridors, and half the Court went with him, for they didn't want to have their stomachs punched—particularly after supper!

They inquired right and left about the marvelous Nightingale, who was known all over the world but had never been heard of by the courtiers in the palace.

At last they found a poor little girl working in the kitchen. She said, "Oh, the Nightingale! I know her well! How beautifully she sings! Every evening I'm allowed to take some scraps of food to my poor sick mother who lives down by the shore. On my way back I feel tired and sit down to rest a moment in the forest, and then I hear the Nightingale! She sounds so

8

beautiful that tears come to my eyes; it's as though Mother were kissing me!"

"Little kitchen maid," said the Chamberlain, "I'll see that you're given a permanent position in the palace kitchen, and you shall even be allowed to watch the Emperor eat his dinner, if only you will lead us to the Nightingale, for we have been ordered to bring her here this evening!"

So, accompanied by half the Court, they set out toward the forest where the Nightingale was usually heard singing. After they had walked some way they heard a cow mooing. "Ah! There she is!" cried the courtiers. "What a powerful voice for such a little creature! But we seem to have heard her before!"

"That's only a cow mooing," said the little kitchen maid. "We still have a good way to go."

Some frogs began croaking in the marshes.

"Lovely!" exclaimed the Court chaplain. "I hear her! She sounds just like little church bells!"

"Those are the frogs croaking," said the kitchen maid. "But we ought to hear her soon."

And then the Nightingale began to sing.

"There she is!" said the little girl. "Listen! Listen! She's up there. Do you see her?" And she pointed to a little gray bird perched high up in the branches.

"Is it possible?" said the Chamberlain. "I never thought she'd look like that! She's so drab and ordinary. . . . But perhaps

9

the sight of so many distinguished people has caused her to lose color!"

"Little Nightingale!" the little kitchen maid called out. "Our gracious Emperor would like to hear you sing!"

"With pleasure!" said the Nightingale, and sang so that it was a joy to hear her.

"It's like the tinkling of crystal bells," said the Chamberlain. "And look at her little throat—how it throbs! It seems odd that we've never heard her before. She'll have a great success at Court!"

"Shall I sing for the Emperor again?" asked the Nightingale, who thought the Emperor must be present.

"Most excellent little Nightingale!" said the Chamberlain. "It is my pleasure to invite you to appear at Court this evening, where you will delight His Imperial Majesty with your enchanting song!"

"It sounds best out in the forest," replied the Nightingale, but she consented to go willingly since it was the Emperor's wish.

The palace had been scrubbed and polished until the walls and the floors, which were made of porcelain, sparkled in the light of thousands of golden lamps. The finest flowers, those with the silver bells on them, were placed in all the corridors. There was such a coming and going, and such a draft, that all the little bells tinkled so loudly you couldn't hear yourself speak.

In the middle of the Great Presence Chamber, where the Em-

12

peror sat on his throne, a golden perch had been placed for the Nightingale. The entire Court was assembled, and the little kitchen maid, who had received the title of Assistant-Cook-to-His-Imperial-Majesty, was allowed to stand behind the door.

The courtiers were dressed in their grandest clothes and they all stared at the little gray bird, to whom the Emperor nodded graciously.

And the Nightingale sang so exquisitely that tears came to the Emperor's eyes and trickled down his cheeks. Then the Nightingale sang even more beautifully—it was enough to melt your heart. The Emperor was so delighted he wanted to give the Nightingale his gold slipper to wear around her neck. But the Nightingale declined the honor with many thanks; she felt she had been sufficiently rewarded.

"I have seen tears in the Emperor's eyes. What could be more precious to me? An Emperor's tears have a mysterious power! I have been amply rewarded!" And she sang again in that sweet, ravishing voice of hers.

"What delightful coquetry!" exclaimed the Court ladies, and they filled their mouths with water and made gurgling sounds in their throats whenever anyone spoke to them. They imagined they were nightingales too! Even the lackeys and the chambermaids admitted to being quite pleased—and that's saying a lot, for they are the most difficult people in the world to satisfy. Yes! The Nightingale was a great success!

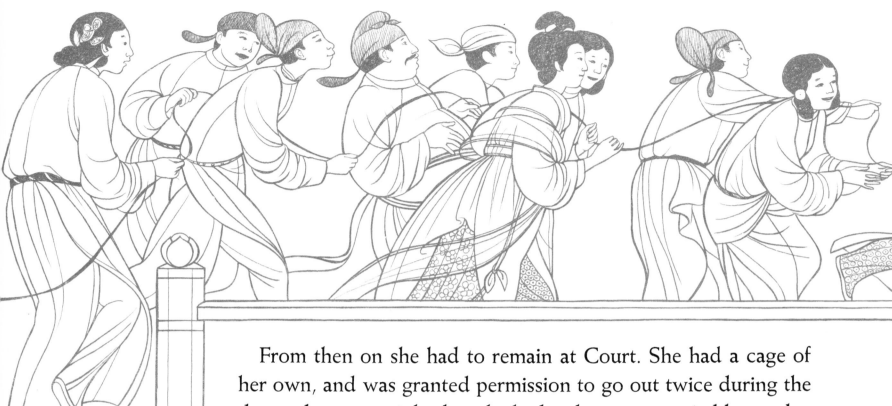

From then on she had to remain at Court. She had a cage of her own, and was granted permission to go out twice during the day and once at night; but she had to be accompanied by twelve servants, who each held on tightly to a silk thread fastened to her leg. There wasn't much fun in that kind of an outing!

The whole city talked of nothing but the wonderful bird, and when two people met, one of them had only to say "Nightin" for the other to say "gale"; then they would sigh in perfect understanding. Eleven shopkeepers' children were named after the Nightingale—but not one of them could sing a note, and they were tone-deaf into the bargain.

One day a large parcel arrived for the Emperor, and on it was written, "Nightingale."

"I expect it's a new book about our famous bird!" said the Emperor; but it wasn't a book at all. It was a wonderful example of the jeweler's art, lying in a velvet-lined case—an artificial nightingale that was supposed to be a copy of the real one, only it was encrusted with diamonds, rubies, and sapphires. When you wound it up, it sang one of the real Nightingale's songs and its tail moved up and down and glittered with silver and gold; around its neck was a little ribbon with the inscription, "The Emperor of Japan's nightingale is poor compared with that of the Emperor of China."

"How marvelous!" they all cried; and the messenger who had brought the artificial bird was immediately given the title of Chief-Imperial-Nightingale-Bringer.

"Now let us hear them sing together—what a duet that will be!"

So they sang together, but it didn't turn out very well, for the Nightingale sang in her own free way, while the artificial bird's song was stilted and mechanical. "The new bird is in no way to blame," said the music master. "It keeps perfect time and obeys all the rules of my special method." Then the artificial bird sang by itself and had just as great a success as the real one. And it was so much more beautiful to look at! It sparkled and shimmered like some fantastic jewel.

It sang its one and only tune thirty-three times without ever getting tired. The courtiers would have liked to hear it over and over again, but the Emperor felt it was the real Nightingale's turn to sing a bit. But where was she? No one had noticed, in all the excitement, that she had flown out of the open window, back to her own green forest.

"Here's a nice state of affairs!" cried the Emperor. The courtiers were all furious and accused the Nightingale of rank ingratitude.

"Well! After all, we still have the better of the two birds!" they said. So the artificial nightingale was made to sing again, and though they now heard the tune for the thirty-fourth time, they still hadn't quite caught on to it—for it was very difficult. The music master was loud in his praise of the artificial bird and said it was much better than the real Nightingale, for its outer covering of diamonds concealed the most delicate and intricate of mechanisms.

"You see, ladies and gentlemen—and, first and foremost, Your Imperial Majesty!—the real Nightingale is totally unpredictable; she sings on the spur of the moment, and there's no way of knowing what you're going to hear. Whereas with the artificial bird everything has been regulated beforehand. You get just what you expect; there are no surprises! The mechanism can be logically explained. You can take the bird apart and examine the intricate wheels and cylinders, how one minute cog fits into another, causing it to sing. It's amazing what human skill and ingenuity are able to accomplish!"

"You're absolutely right!" they all agreed, and the very next Sunday the music master was authorized to demonstrate the bird to the common people. "They must hear it sing too," said the Emperor. So they did hear it and were so delighted they seemed quite intoxicated, as though they'd drunk too much tea—for that's what the Chinese drink, you know. They all exclaimed, "Oh!" held up their forefingers, and nodded their heads. But the poor fisherman who had heard the real Nightingale sing said, "Yes! It's pretty enough; it's a fairly good imitation, but there's something lacking—I can't explain just what it is!"

The real Nightingale was banished from the Empire.

The artificial bird was kept on a silk cushion by the Emperor's bed. Around it were placed all the presents that had been sent to it, all made of gold and precious stones. Its title had been raised to High-Imperial-Bedside-Table-Singer, First-Class-on-the-Left.

The Emperor considered the side nearer his heart to be the more distinguished—for an Emperor's heart is on the left, like everybody else's.

The music master wrote five-and-twenty tomes about the artificial bird, so long-winded and so learned and so full of the most complicated phrases that though everybody read them no one could understand a word; but of course they didn't dare admit it—they didn't want to appear stupid, for that would have meant having their stomachs punched, and they didn't like the thought of that!

In this way a whole year passed. By now the Emperor, the Court, and all the Chinese people knew every note and every trill of the artificial bird's song, and they enjoyed it all the more for that; now they were able to join in the singing, which of course they did. Even the street urchins sang, "Zeezee, zee! Gloo, gloo, gloo!" and the Emperor sang it too. It was all perfectly delightful!

But one evening, when the artificial bird was singing away and the Emperor lay on his bed listening to it, something went "crack!" inside the bird—a spring had broken. There was a great whirring of wheels, and the song stopped.

The Emperor leaped out of bed and sent for his personal physician, but there was nothing he could do! So a watchmaker was summoned, and after a great deal of talk and a long and careful examination, he managed to fix the mechanism fairly well, but he said it shouldn't be used too often, as many of the cogs had worn down and would be almost impossible to replace. He couldn't guarantee that the song would ever be the same again. It was a tragic state of affairs! Only once a year was the artificial bird allowed to sing—and even that put quite a strain on it. But the music master made a little speech, full of complicated words, declaring that the song was just as good as ever; and of course that settled it. Everyone agreed it was just as good as ever!

Five more years went by, and the whole country was heavy with grief—for the people were devoted to their Emperor, and now he was sick and the doctors said he hadn't long to live.

A new Emperor had already been chosen, and the people stood outside in the street and asked the Chamberlain if there was any hope of their old Emperor getting well again.

"Peh!" said the Chamberlain, and shook his head.

The Emperor lay in his huge, magnificent bed, so cold and so pale that the courtiers thought him already dead, and they all dashed off to pay court to the new Emperor. The lackeys ran outside to gossip about it, and the chambermaids gave a large tea party. Thick felt had been laid down on the floors of all the halls and corridors to muffle the sound of footsteps; the palace was as quiet as a tomb. But the Emperor wasn't dead yet. He lay there stiff and pale in his magnificent bed with the long velvet hangings and the heavy gold tassels. High up in the wall was an open window through which the moon shone down on him and on the artificial bird by his side.

The poor Emperor could hardly breathe; he felt something heavy weighing on his chest; he opened his eyes and saw that it was Death. He was wearing the Emperor's gold crown, and held the gold sword of state in one hand and the Imperial banner in the other; and from the folds of the heavy velvet hangings strange faces peered out—some hideous and evil, and others mild and gentle. They were the Emperor's good and bad deeds watching him as he lay there with Death weighing on his heart.

"Do you remember this?" they whispered to him one after another. "Do you remember that?" And they reminded him of many, many things—and the sweat stood out on his brow.

"I never knew about all that!" cried the Emperor. "Music! Music!" he shouted. "Strike up the great Chinese gong and drown out their voices!"

But the voices continued, and Death nodded his head, like a real Chinese, in agreement with all that was said.

"Music! Music!" the Emperor cried again. "Precious little golden bird, sing to me! Sing! I implore you, sing! I've showered you with gold and precious jewels. I even hung my gold slipper around your neck with my own hands. Sing to me now! Sing!"

But the bird was silent. It couldn't sing unless it was wound up, but there was no one there to do it. Death kept on staring at the Emperor with his great hollow eyes, and the silence grew more and more terrifying.

Suddenly, through the window, came the sound of an exquisite

28

song. It was the little, living Nightingale perched on a branch outside. She had heard of the Emperor's suffering and had come to bring him hope and comfort with her song. As she sang the phantoms gradually faded away, the blood began to flow more swiftly through the Emperor's feeble body, and Death himself listened and said, "Keep on singing, little Nightingale! Keep on!"

"Yes! If you will give me the golden sword! If you will give me the Imperial banner! If you will give me the Emperor's golden crown!"

And Death gave up the treasures one by one for each song the Nightingale sang. She sang of the peaceful churchyard where the white roses bloom, where the air is sweet with the scent of the elder tree, and where the green grass is moistened by the tears of those who have lost their loved ones. And, as he listened, Death was filled with a great longing to be back in his own garden, and he vanished out of the window like a cold white mist.

"Thank you, thank you!" said the Emperor. "You heavenly little bird—I know you now! I chased you out of my country, out of my Empire. And with your song you have chased the hateful dreams from around my bed; you have driven Death from my heart. How can I ever repay you, lovely bird?"

"You have repaid me," said the Nightingale. "The very first time I sang to you, you gave me your tears—I shall never forget that! Those are the jewels that gladden a singer's heart. But go to sleep now, and wake up well and strong! I'll sing to you!"

29

The Nightingale sang, and the Emperor fell into a deep sleep; a gentle, refreshing sleep.

When he awoke the next morning the sun was shining through the window, and he felt well and strong again; none of his servants had come back to him, for they thought he was dead, but the Nightingale was still singing.

"You must never leave me!" cried the Emperor. "You need only sing when you feel like singing, and I shall smash the artificial bird into a thousand pieces."

"Don't do that!" said the Nightingale. "It did the best it could! Keep it with you. I can't settle down and live here in the palace, but let me come and go as I like. I'll sit on the branch outside your window and sing to you, so that your thoughts may be serene and joyful; I'll sing of happy people and of those who suffer; I'll sing of the good and evil all around you which is kept hidden from you; for the little songbird flies far and wide—to the poor fisherman, and the peasant in his hut, to all those who are far away from you and from your Court. I love your heart much better than your crown, yet I venerate your crown, for there is an aura of sanctity about it! I shall come and sing for you—but one thing you must promise me!"

"Anything!" said the Emperor, who stood there in his Imperial robes, which he had put on all by himself, holding the heavy golden sword against his heart.

"I ask only one thing of you: Let no one know you have a little bird who tells you everything. It will be much better so!"

And the Nightingale flew away.

The servants and the courtiers came in to attend their dead Emperor. They were struck dumb with amazement when they saw him standing there; and the Emperor said to them, "Good morning!"